Wet Dog!

by Elise Broach

illustrations by David Catrow

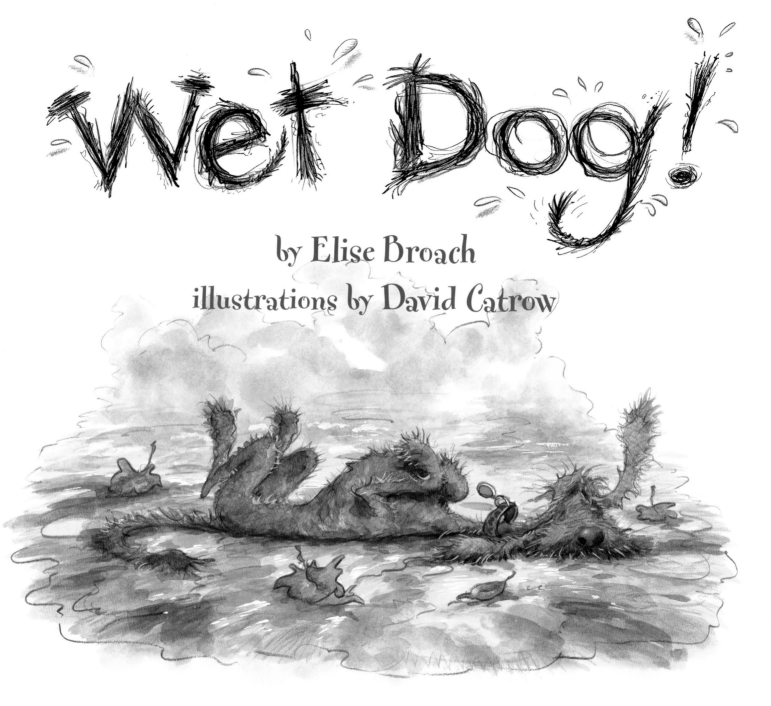

Dial Books for Young Readers New York

For Grace
—E.B.

To Goobie, the mustache man
—D.C.

DIAL BOOKS FOR YOUNG READERS
A division of Penguin Young Readers Group • Published by The Penguin Group
Penguin Group (USA) Inc., 375 Hudson Street, New York, NY 10014, U.S.A.
Penguin Group (Canada), 10 Alcorn Avenue, Toronto, Ontario, Canada M4V 3B2 (a division of Pearson Penguin Canada Inc.)
Penguin Books Ltd, 80 Strand, London WC2R 0RL, England
Penguin Ireland, 25 St. Stephen's Green, Dublin 2, Ireland (a division of Penguin Books Ltd)
Penguin Group (Australia), 250 Camberwell Road, Camberwell, Victoria 3124, Australia (a division of Pearson Australia Group Pty Ltd)
Penguin Books India Pvt Ltd, 11 Community Centre, Panchsheel Park, New Delhi - 110 017, India
Penguin Group (NZ), Cnr Airborne and Rosedale Roads, Albany, Auckland 1310, New Zealand (a division of Pearson New Zealand Ltd)
Penguin Books (South Africa) (Pty) Ltd, 24 Sturdee Avenue, Rosebank, Johannesburg 2196, South Africa
Penguin Books Ltd, Registered Offices: 80 Strand, London WC2R 0RL, England
Text copyright © 2005 by Elise Broach
Illustrations copyright © 2005 by David Catrow
Designed by Lily Malcom
Text set in New Hampshire
Manufactured in China on acid-free paper
10 9 8 7 6 5 4 3 2 1

Library of Congress Cataloging-in-Publication Data
Broach, Elise.
  Wet dog! / by Elise Broach ; illustrations by David Catrow.
     p. cm.
Summary: A dog's attempts to cool off on a hot day get him into trouble and finally lead him to disrupt a country wedding.
  ISBN 0-8037-2809-3
[1. Dogs—Fiction. 2. Heat—Fiction. 3. Country life—Fiction.] I. Catrow, David, ill. II. Title.
PZ7.B78083We 2005
[E]—dc22   2003014150

The art was created using pencil and watercolor.

*H*e was a good old dog and a hot
old dog, as he lay in the noonday sun.
And he dozed and he drowsed in the
beating-down sun, with his long pink
tongue hanging out.

Well, that too-hot dog in the too-hot
sun just had to cool off somehow. So
he heaved to his feet, and he sniffed
the air, and he trotted off down the
road . . .

pat-a-pat, pat-a-pat, pat.

And that's when he saw a man washing a car,
a long black, shiny black car.

Old dog stepped in the soft, cool stream till the wet soaked through to his skin. Then he shook and he shook with a happy-dog smile, wagging his happy-dog tail . . . shaky-shake, shaky-shake, shake!

"Wet dog!" cried the man with the shiny black car. "Shoo! Go on now, shoo!"

Wet dog smiled his sorry-dog smile and wagged his sorry-dog tail.
Then he flapped his ears, and he sniffed the air, and he trotted off
down the road . . . pat-a-pat, pat-a-pat, pat.

And that's when he saw a lady washing some pans, some piled-high, sticky-high pans.

Wet dog stepped in the splash and the suds till the cool flowed down his fur.

Then he shook and he shook with a happy-dog smile, wagging his happy-dog tail . . .

shaky-shake, shaky-shake, shake!

"Wet dog!" cried the lady with the sticky-high pans. "Shoo! Go on now, shoo!"

Wet dog smiled his sorry-dog smile and wagged his sorry-dog tail.
Then he flapped his ears, and he sniffed the air, and he trotted off
down the road . . . pat-a-pat, pat-a-pat, pat.

And that's when he saw a lady spraying some blooms, some pale pink, petal pink blooms.

Wet dog stepped in the sparkling spray, and the soft mist cooled his face. Then he shook and he shook with a happy-dog smile, wagging his happy-dog tail . . . shaky-shake, shaky-shake, shake!

"Wet dog!" cried the lady with the petal pink blooms. "Shoo! Go on now, shoo!"

Wet dog smiled his sorry-dog smile and wagged his sorry-dog tail.
Then he flapped his ears, and he sniffed the air, and he trotted off
down the road . . . pat-a-pat, pat-a-pat, pat.

And that's when he saw some men playing a song, a singing-loud, dancing-loud song. Wet dog stood by the side of the creek, feeling the music rise.

Then he danced right into the trickle and the muck with his big, soft paws sinking in.

And he shook and he shook with a happy-dog smile, wagging his happy-dog tail . . . shaky-shake, shaky-shake, shake!

"Wet dog!" cried the men with the dancing-loud song.
"Shoo! Go on now, shoo!"

Wet dog smiled his sorry-dog smile and wagged his sorry-dog tail.
Then he flapped his ears, and he sniffed the air, and he trotted off
down the road . . . pat-a-pat, pat-a-pat, pat.

That's when he came to a lake.

Now, there by the shore in the beating-down sun were people in fine, fancy clothes. There were ladies in curls, men in bow ties, babies in soft, flouncy hats. Wet dog stood by the lake, and he looked at the crowd in the too-too-too-hot sun.

Then he stepped right into the shimmering cool of that whoo-cool, too-cool lake. And he splished and he splashed in the rippling waves, and he bounded back onto the shore.

He was wet to the bone, so he shook and he shook . . .
shaky-shake, shaky-shake, shake!

"Wet dog!" cried the people in their fine, fancy clothes.

"Shoo! Go on now, SHOOOOOOO!"

But wet dog shook with his
ears flying fast, and his wet
fur spray-spray-spraying.

And a baby just laughed. She was a fine, fancy baby, in too-hot clothes, with the water fresh on her face. She laughed and she laughed, clapping her hands at the wet-dog rain in the air.

"More!" cried the baby, arms open wide. "More, dog, more, dog! More!"

Then the people laughed too.

And they danced and they dove and they splashed and they strode into the blue-cool, oooo-cool water.

Well, they splashed and they danced—how they splashed and they danced!—as the sun slid low in the sky. And they patted wet dog from his ears to his tail . . .

"Hoo-ray, wet dog!
Hoo-ray!"